¶ Structure, Style, and Truth

Structure, Style, and Truth

ELEMENTS OF THE SHORT STORY

John M. Daniel

FITHIAN PRESS, SANTA BARBARA, 1998

Printed in the United States of America

Published by Fithian Press
A division of Daniel and Daniel, Publishers, Inc.
Post Office Box 1525
Santa Barbara, CA 93102

Book design: Eric Larson

LIBRARY OF CONGRESS CATALOGING-IN-PUBLICATION DATA
Daniel, John, 1941–
Structure, style, and truth : elements of the short story / John M. Daniel.
p. cm.
ISBN 1-56474-272-5 (alk. paper)
1. Fiction—Authorship. 2. Short story. I. Title
PN3373.D26 1998
808.3'1—dc21 98-14825
CIP

CONTENTS

¶ Structure, Style, and Truth

¶ Introduction

The short story is arguably the oldest art form in human culture. As long as we have had language, we have used that language, combined with imagination, to entertain each other with tales. After a long day at work, which in prehistoric, hunter-gatherer times meant physical toil and danger as well, people came together to relax in the security of each other's company. I imagine they bragged about what they had done that day, or remembered even more exciting days. The stories they told around their campfires got retold and embellished—polished, edited. True accounts grew into entertaining, believable lies, and the short story was born.

So were authors. The tellers of tales found they enjoyed having an audience, and consciously or unconsciously they competed for time in the firelight. It became clear quickly that whoever could tell the most entertaining tales would be allowed to tell the most tales. So even before we had written language, we were inventing the craft of writing. We were either inventing or discovering (the question is a matter of thorny philosophical debate) the rules of fiction.

The short story has come a long way in the millennia between those days and these. In various aspects the art form has changed with the times and has been adapted to fit the cultures of different eras and different places. But there are a few defining truths about the short story form that have lasted throughout human history, from which experimental deviations have been only short-lived. Looking at the common features of short stories from all time, we can make a working definition of what a short story is. We can also come up with some dependable opinions on why some stories are better than others. Thus we can come up with an arguable but defendable set of "rules" for short fiction.

This book lists a number of these rules, divided into three categories: rules about style, rules about structure, and rules about truth. The second part of the book has six short essays on how these rules can apply to six specific types of short stories. The last part of the book offers a few techniques for completing the process: having your stories read by others.

This book does not come with a guarantee that you will be a great writer or that your stories will be published and make you money and fame. But I do promise you that if you think about what you're doing while you write your stories, you'll enjoy the process more, you'll probably write better, and you'll have a better chance of seeing your work in print. This small book will help you think about what is involved in the very challenging and satisfying art form called the short story.

¶ What is a Short Story?

A short story is a series of words. As readers we usually meet this series of words on the pages of a book or magazine; as writers we usually see the story as a growing stack of paper, a manuscript in progress. What makes a short story different from a novel is its brevity; what makes it different from an article is its fiction (or in some cases its fictional technique).

WHAT DOES "SHORT" MEAN?

The length, or brevity, of a short story is somewhat flexible. Generally a short story is at least five hundred words long, and any story longer than ten thousand words long has outgrown the form and entered the realm of novella. There's no reason why one length is better than another, but for economic reasons there are very few magazines that will publish any story longer than five thousand words; and any story under fifteen hundred words is now often labeled a "short-short" and treated as a curiosity. I once published a collection of very good stories, each of them only fifty-five words long. But those stories were freaks. In any case, the most successful short story gives a reader a reason to sit in a chair for a pleasant while and will compel the reader to stay in that chair until the story is read. I propose four thousand words as a satisfying model length from which to vary upwards or downwards.

WHAT DOES "STORY" MEAN?

The word "story" is harder to define, and I will rely on the rest of this chapter to serve as a description rather than a definition of fiction. Better yet, the lion's share of this book is made up of good principles, which are better than descriptions or definitions. (Show, don't tell.)

Still, I can posit a necessary ingredient of a short story, and it's this: something happens to someone. I borrow that tenet from Rust Hills, who phrases it slightly differently, and from John D. MacDonald, who says it still differently. Something happens to someone. A simple statement, but a statement full of business.

What happens? Something important. Often danger. Usually desire. Probably a choice. And a consequence of that choice. You can expect a change. In any case, *something*. Something happens to someone.

Someone? Who? Every story has a different someone, but the point is it's *someone*. Short stories are about people. They're about the human condition.

They're not about nobody. They're about somebody. Something happens to someone.

WHAT DOES A SHORT STORY LOOK LIKE?

A short story looks like this:

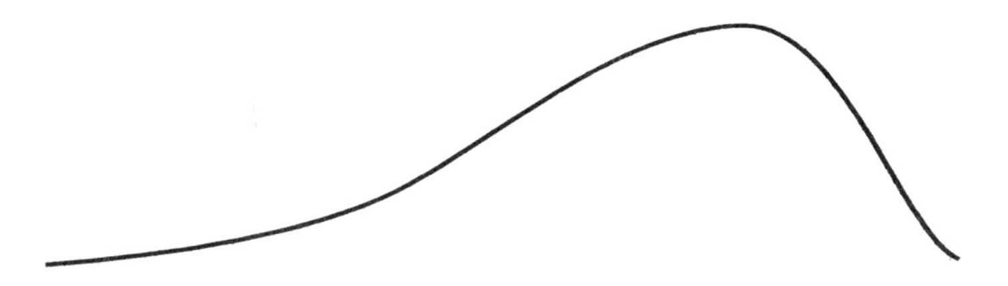

I don't mean to say that all short stories are alike, that they all have the same shape. But there is something true about the drawing I've just given. This is the path taken by the successful short story, and by every other art form that's linear, that requires a journey through time. They all get more and more exciting as they go along, more compelling, more engaging, stronger and stronger until they reach a climax, after which they resoundingly relax.

Sound familiar? It should. We're talking about the creative act here: sex. That should not surprise you, nor should it embarrass you. The art of the short story, like the art of the novel or the symphony or the movie or the popular song or myth or ballet, is to take someone through a passage of time that becomes more and more engaging until it's gone as far as it can possibly go. This is the way pleasure works. It is the way creation works.

The answers are simple and complex, full of balance and irony.

A short story *preaches:* like all art, a story is made to make us better people. But because a story shouldn't be as dull as a Calvinist sermon or a Maoist opera, a story gets its message across by *entertaining,* entertaining so well that the preaching is hidden in camouflage.

A story *observes the truth.* I would say "tells the truth," but that would be stating the obvious, and it's not always the obvious that the story observes. But it always finds truth and observes it. How? By telling lies. That's what fiction is, after all: *prevarication.*

A story *looks within.* As if with a microscope, short stories look into our pockets, our closets, our secrets, our psyches to find out why we do what we do. At the same time, a short story *explores the universe* as if with a telescope, presenting to the reader a gift of wisdom and knowledge brought back from the writer's journey.

Preach. Entertain. Observe truth. Prevaricate. Look within. Explore the universe.

Make an acronym out of that list, and you'll find out what stories are all about, and why they're so simple, and so complex.

¶ Rules for Writing Good Short Stories

As a reader and as a writer, and as an editor and as a publisher, I have met thousands of short stories. I assure you that some of them have been better than others. I have come to believe that there are consistent reasons why some stories work (or play) better than others. I choose to call those reasons, those dependable reasons, "rules."

You may not wish to follow these rules as you write your own stories, but you should at least be aware of them, and know that if you're not following them, you are not following them by choice. If you do find yourself following them, it won't be by choice. It will be because you are writing well.

If you don't believe that art should have rules, then think of what follows as a set of standards, or a collection of common sense. If what follows doesn't make sense to you, then you may be a very good writer, but you are not a short-story writer in any sense I understand.

RULES ABOUT STYLE

¶ Show 'em, don't tell 'em.

¶ Stay in control: outline your story, and follow your outline.

¶ Stay in control: don't be controlled by your outline. Allow yourself to be surprised by your characters and what they do. Write to find out what happens next.

¶ If those last two items seem to contradict one another, you're right, so find the rule that works best for you, but remember that the desired result is the same: a story that presents an ironic combination of inevitability and surprise. However you get there, you must end with a satisfying, strongly constructed, seamless story.

¶ Be selective. Edgar Allan Poe, one of the principle architects of modern short fiction, insisted that every element, every word even, of a short story must contribute to the harmonious whole. Poe was right. Put into the story only those elements of character, plot, and setting that are relevant to what the story does. Anything else is fat. Be selective, and select no fat. And be sure to edit out anything you put into the story just to show off. As Faulkner said, delete "your darlings."

¶ Being selective is especially important when

you're writing autobiographical fiction or even just writing from personal experience (which is inevitable). Remember that what was significant to you may not be relevant to the story. If that's the case, save it for another story where it will fit better.

¶ Watch your step with point of view. A good rule for point of view in short stories is one is enough. Multiple points of view are okay, but the more you have the harder it is to do it right. The hard-and-fast rule is that whenever you're in one point of view, that's the only point of view you're in.

¶ Write strong. Verb constructions are stronger than noun constructions. The active voice is stronger than the passive voice. Every noun does not need an adjective. Reexamine every adverb and throw away at least half of them, especially those that end in "ly," and almost all of the ones that end in "ly" to modify how a character has just said a line of dialogue.

¶ Keep writing strong. Choose strong words: short, Anglo-Saxon words are much stronger than long, Latinate words. Choose the right word, and not, as Mark Twain cautioned us, "its second cousin." Write lean, because extra, unnecessary words get in the way and weaken your story.

¶ Avoid the habitual past, and get right to the direct, moving action. A story has to hit the ground running. The first sentence in the story should be the best sentence in the story.

¶ End the story gloriously. The last sentence in the story should be the best sentence in the story.
¶ Have I just contradicted myself? Can there be more than one best sentence in a story? Maybe not mathematically, but you should try for it, and you should throw in another at the climax, and a few more during the buildup of tension. Let your story be peppered with best sentences.
¶ Irony is a major ingredient of writing at the sentence level. It means surprise. Use surprising, unexpected words and put them together in original ways that mean even more than they say.
¶ Caution: don't overwrite. Don't write fancy. Watch out for five-dollar words. It's a thin line, but don't show off, even when your fingers are dancing on the keys, celebrating the pleasure of words. How do you write with the grace of Fred Astaire without being a showoff? Perhaps the best advice comes from Hemingway: be honest. And be honest more consistently than Hemingway.
¶ Reexamine the last sentence of every paragraph, the last paragraph of every scene, and the last scene of every story. Does it just summarize what's already been shown in the action? If so, dump the summary. End your paragraphs, scenes, and stories with action, not reflection.

¶ Tell a story. Something has to happen to someone. That may seem to go without saying, but remember that a story without plot is like a meal without food.

¶ The story starts at the beginning. It must hit the ground running. (Have I said that before?) The first sentence in the story must be the best sentence in the story. Don't begin with a weather report unless the weather is essential to the plot. Watch out for one character alone for too many pages at the beginning of the story; you (or your character) may get lost in thought and forget to have something happen.

¶ Remember Chekhov's loaded rifle. Applying that rule to short stories, if there's a loaded rifle in an early scene, it must go off in or before the last scene of the story. Conversely, if a bomb goes off at the end of the story, chances are that bomb is in large measure what the story's about, and it must be planted, ticking, early in the story.

¶ Don't be overly predictable. Surprise. Irony is an essential ingredient of plot construction. Irony at the plot level is the unexpected event that makes perfect sense. Make the reader react with "AHA!"—not with "Duh." or "Huh?"

¶ The beginning of a story has to make the reader want to read the middle of the story. The well-worn phrase that wears well is, "Hook 'em with curiosity, and hold 'em with conflict."

¶ Conflict is an absolute necessity of fiction short or long. Otherwise, what's the difference? The short story assumes there are obstacles to overcome, differences to reconcile, winners vs. losers, good guys vs. bad guys, inner struggles, arguments, fistfights, car chases, or merely difficult decisions. Mild or major, the conflict is at the heart of both character and plot. And somewhere in the plot, this conflict often results in a significant shift in the balance of power.

¶ Which means: stories are about change. When we say "something happens to someone," we're talking about a change.

¶ Often—perhaps more often than just often—that change is the result of a choice. A character must make a choice, and because of that choice, the character changes.

¶ Built into that last statement is the concept of consequence. Consequence makes all the difference when it comes to plot. Vladimir Nabokov's wonderful, simple example shows the difference between a plot and a mere sequence of events. The latter: "The King died and the Queen died." The former: "The King died, and the Queen died of grief." A plot is not just a sequence of events: A, then B, then C, then D. A plot says B happened as a result of A, and that because of B, C had to happen, which led (surprisingly or inevitably or both) to D, and so on. Until...

¶ *Climax!* Need I say more?

¶ More: Resolution, or reverberation, or relaxation. Stories usually let the reader relax a bit after the climax. That's kind of them, but the story shouldn't just roll over and go to sleep. Keep the story alive to the end, and make the last sentence the best one in the story.

RULES ABOUT TRUTH

¶ Be significant. The reason stories are important is because they're about what's important. That doesn't mean that all stories must be about love and death (although the finest stories are about one or the other and the finest of all are about both). But they must be about things that matter. The things that happen to your characters have to be important to the reader, because they're important to you, because they're things that matter in terms of the human condition.

¶ Significance is important for its entertainment value: desire, danger, quest, and change.

¶ Significance is also important for its moral value: we create art in order to make this a better planet for ourselves, our fellow human beings, and our fellow species. If you don't believe that, or if you think it's too grand a challenge, let me go further and say that all we do in life is for that purpose, and art (in this case writing short fiction) is but a concentrated effort in the grand cause.

¶ Lighten up. Have fun with your writing. Art

is for play, after all, and for God's sake, don't put your readers to sleep. You should indeed write about matters that are socially significant, but avoid sermons, and remember that fiction is primarily about people, not about ideas.

¶ Speaking of significance, things that are not significant are laundry lists (a generic term not always referring to clothing), weather reports, and stories about writers. Also gratuitous sex. Sex is fine (you better believe it), but it must be important to the story and its plot and its theme and its characters, and not there just for the fun of it. The act itself, in the story, has to have a reason to be there in terms of fiction: it illustrates a character, or better yet, advances the plot by changing a relationship.

¶ Respect your reader's intelligence. Imagine that your reader is at least as intelligent as you. Don't explain your story; if you're afraid your reader won't get it, you need to do some rewriting. Don't tell your reader what to think; persuade your reader to think a certain way by how you write.

¶ Avoid gimmicks. Don't overpunctuate!!!!! Don't use phony phonetics (sez I). These aren't just matters of style; they're matters of honesty.

¶ Write with authority; that's why you're called an author. That means, as we've been told forever, write about what you know about. This does not mean you must travel the globe like Richard Haliburton or participate in every sport like George Plimpton before you can write. If you think the things you already know about are not important enough, you're mistaken. Writing about what you know about does not mean you can't set your stories in foreign lands you've never visited, or far-off planets, for that matter. It means that what the story is really about is its emotional content, the part that comes from within you, and that's something you can't lie about. Write what you know, and tell the truth.

¶ Do research so you won't be embarrassed by mistakes, but don't let research turn your lively fiction into a dull catalog of facts.

¶ Use your imagination, and lie. But even then, tell the truth about it. Remember that a story about a struggle between blobs and robots, set on Pluto in 2356, is really about human life on Earth today.

¶ Don't be afraid of the dark. I encourage you to write about troublesome things. That doesn't mean you can't write about love and laughter, but you should also realize that all good stories about relationships are about the problems in relationships, and that all humor comes from pain and suffering.

¶ Respect your characters. Stories are about people, not about symbols. You and your reader must spend time with these characters, so make them individual and interesting. Love these people, even the rotters; they have a lot to tell you. Show (don't tell) what they're like, and let them speak and think for themselves. Let your readers draw their own conclusions about these people; if you've shown the characters in action, you don't have to worry about how the reader will judge them.

¶ Dialogue has to sound like real people talking. They may be outrageous people, and they may say outrageous things, but only the dullest people speak in clichés, and the dullest people are seldom worth writing or reading about. Another thing that real people don't do is pack their conversations full of plot information.

¶ Read your words aloud. Be prepared to be embarrassed, and if you're embarrassed because something sounds phony, you have some rewriting to do.

¶ All writers rewrite. If you're satisfied with your first draft, you're not an artist. That's not writing. As Capote quipped to Kerouac, that's just typing.

¶ You may break the rules. In fact, you should break the rules. And when you break the rules, do so on purpose and out loud, because breaking the rules is part of what your story is about.

¶ The one rule you may not break is this:

¶ Your motto shall be: LET ME ENTERTAIN YOU.

This of course is only a sketchy introduction to the theory of short fiction, but it will serve. The rules that I've just listed, and many more that I haven't, have served the art form for millennia, since stories were first swapped around the primal campfire. They have withstood history, human fads and fashions, and even television (don't get me started), and they will survive far into the future, regardless of how technology may complicate the way stories are distributed from mind to mind.

¶ Six Common Types of Short Stories, and How to Write them Right

AUTOBIOGRAPHICAL SHORT STORIES

Many autobiographical stories concern rites of passage. Rites of passage are changes we all go through. Although we may not experience them in exactly the same way, in any society there are some experiences that are common to most of its members. These happen periodically, throughout our lives. The important thing about these shared experiences, in terms of short fiction, is not that they happen (because by their nature there's nothing unusual about them), but the psychological changes that happen because of them, which are as different as the people they happen to. They are called rites of passage, a term borrowed from anthropology, because they mark a change from one psychological "place" to the next.

A case can be made that all fiction is autobiographical. Just as we can assume that any adult who writes about childhood has experienced childhood in some form, it's a fairly sure bet that anyone writing convincingly about troubled marriage is, or has been, married; and even if the writer's marriage is or was quite happy, the writer knows from experience what hard work marriage can sometimes be. Even writers deliberately writing about things they've never done are drawing on their own experience. A story that takes the reader through a swamp full of hungry crocodiles draws on the writer's knowledge of danger, perhaps learned during his first day in a new school or her first time driving on a metropolitan freeway.

But for the purpose of this discussion, autobiographical stories draw on real memories of real events.

There's nobody in the world who doesn't have memories worth writing about. Flannery O'Connor said, "Anybody who has survived his childhood has enough information about life to last him the rest of his days." The difference between writers and the rest of humanity is that writers almost automatically tend to translate their experience into art, usually in retrospect. We artists tend to process our universe, turning chaos into transcendent order. Perhaps that's what keeps us sane; perhaps it's just our way of being nuts. Either way, we must do it.

And so we write about what we know about. We write about our first family, our parents, and we talk about the havoc wreaked by the Oedipal conflict, and we talk about the the generation gap, which opens the first time we discover that our gods are human beings. We write about our siblings—our first friends, our first rivals. Friendships rewarding and sour, and love in all its inevitable forms—romantic, sexual, explosive or enduring. Courtship, marriage, decay and divorce. We write about the second family, the one with our own children, and the generation gap that reopens when we realize we've mistakenly created monsters instead of angels. We write about critical moments large and small: toilet training, summer camp, bar mitzvah, first menstruation, the accident that happened the day after getting our first driver's license, discovering sex, anorexia, getting eyeglasses, sacrificing friendship for tin trophies, an abortion, being born again, finding your politics, turning to crime, going to war, passing the bar, the death of a best friend, the death of a child, the loss of a love, the fall from grace, being promoted, the painful change of attitudes, the birth of a grandchild, the death of a marriage, the rebirth of your youth, crippling illness, retirement, the final adventure that lies ahead.

These are just a few of the moments in life that work as the beginnings of short stories. Anyone who reads this list has gone through at least a few of them, and everyone who reads this list has heard or read stories about all of them. We all have stories to tell, stories from our past, stories that others will easily relate to.

On the other hand, just because we've all had lives does not mean that the memories of our experiences will translate to good fiction if only we write them down. It's not just a matter of having a good memory. The process of writing autobiographical fiction is more complicated, more artistic than mere oral history. Here are some techniques that do the magic of translating narration into dramatization, and some common ingredients of successful autobiographical short stories.

The autobiographical story should subtly inform the reader when the story took place with respect to the history of the world. Since different eras have different values and expectations that play on the events and their consequences, it's important to know what atmosphere is involved. You can establish time with an actual event, a news flash, or you can establish the era more generally, in terms of customs or social trends.

It's also important to let your reader know where you were in your life's journey. That can be a simple matter of stating an age or it can be shown by details. The more important change, as we've seen, is not a matter of age or physical development, but the milestone marked by the outcome of the story. This is the milestone that is unique to your character/yourself. By saying how old you were when the events happened, you find a link with your reader (who has been that same age, presumably, or can expect to be); by telling how your experience was your own, you're giving the reader something new.

Keep in mind three words that begin with S: Selection, Significance, and Style.

Your personal history will get you nowhere if you're not artfully selective about what you include. Don't try to tell everything about your life; you'll end up with a story as tiresome to read as it was to write. Instead, decide what the story is really about and use only the details that apply.

A story, any story, should be significant, and the significance should transcend your personal experience and growth. The significant aspect of a story should challenge the reader to think and to learn something new about the human condition.

The importance of style almost goes without saying, because if you enjoy writing, you enjoy doing it well. You treasure irony, and you love choosing the right words and placing them in the right order. You know that your story must not reek of overwriting, but you also have confidence that your reader wants to hear the sound of your voice.

The main difference between oral history and autobiographical fiction, of course, lies in the word "fiction," with all it implies. I just said it's more than having a good memory; now I'll say good fiction requires the ability to forget what really happened from time to time. The most amateurish defense of an unsuccessful scene is "but that's the way it really happened." So what? You have permission to tell lies if doing so makes a better story. You'll still be true to the lessons learned in life.

Caution: writing autobiographical fiction can be dangerous to your health. If you write about your family, don't show your family the story until it's already in print, and even then you can expect to hear such comments as: "That's not the way it really happened," "Uncle Dwight was *not* a drunk," "You might have mentioned that my second marriage was much happier," or "You weren't that easy to live with either." They'll think they're looking at snapshots from Thanksgiving, and they're probably the kind of relatives who think any picture taken of them is unflattering.

Another reason to embrace the lie.

Don't be gratuitously unkind, and remember that your stories may also celebrate the joy of your experience and the heroes of your past as well as the hard lessons learned. Be sure to let your family see those positive stories as well, but even then, it will be safer if you wait until they're in print.

But write your stories anyway. Change the details if you need to keep your family happy. Change names. Turn men into women, the women into men, and set the stories in Indianapolis. Throw in a few nice things about your ex-spouse, even if they're not true. The important truth will come through, and if your friends and family can't live with that important truth, tough.

From whom do they think you learned that truth anyway?

SOCIALLY SIGNIFICANT SHORT STORIES

This article is about fiction that deals with social issues, by which I mean the problems of society. "Social issues," in this discussion, does not refer to manners and customs, but to the grander business of how people in groups treat each other, through government or other forms of social control. Politics, not politesse.

Fiction has dealt with social and political issues since the beginning of writing, and probably long before that. Many of our myths—including that of the Garden of Eden—are about social contract and conduct, and those myths, in addition to being good stories in their own right, have served as models for important fiction ever since. Inspired by myths, or just moved by the human condition, writers (and other artists) have been examining the system as long as there has been a system.

Writers of conscience through the ages have done their part to force readers to think hard about such important issues as crime and punishment, war and peace, health and aging, equitable economics, the fragile environment, racism, sexism, and a host of other thorny matters that we have had to deal with ever since our first parents first tasted apples.

Any well-read lover of fiction would probably enjoy the exercise of naming the ten "greatest" writers of all time, whether that means the ten "best," or the ten "most important." Go ahead, try it. I suggest we eliminate living writers, because one of the tests of greatness is immortality; and to keep it simple I suggest we stick with writers in the English language. You have to come up with your own list, and I won't force you to accept my candidates, but I think you should at least consider: Jonathan Swift, Charles

Dickens, Mark Twain, D. H. Lawrence, Sinclair Lewis, George Orwell, Aldous Huxley, John Steinbeck, James Baldwin, and Wallace Stegner for starters. This list is loaded for the point of my argument, and I admit these aren't all favorite authors of mine, but I do believe they're all immortal, and that readers will find wisdom in their books forever, no matter how societies may change.

The first point I want to make about these writers, and I expect the same point could be made of half the candidates in any good list of ten immortal writers, is that they were concerned to the point of fervor with the problems of society.

The second point to make is that the sociopolitical works for which these fiction writers are best known are novels, not short stories. There are some short story writers in the list, but most people can name more Lawrence novels than Lawrence stories, and when they think of Steinbeck's short stories they think of intriguing interpersonal relationships rather than the sweeping social challenges of *The Grapes of Wrath*.

In other words, as important as social and political issues are to the art of fiction, they're not especially common to the art of *short* fiction. It appears that the short story is not a terribly effective tool for saving the world. It is true that much good political and social short fiction has been written. But most memorable sociopolitical fiction has shown up in novels, and society and politics are relatively low on the scorecard of issues that motivate short stories.

Why is that? Probably because matters of sweeping social change need more room than five thousand words. Short stories tend to focus on the moment, not the era. On the person, not the People. On psychology rather than sociology.

Having made the point that short fiction is not often primarily concerned with social and political issues, with saving the world, let me now do an apparent U-turn and say that nearly all good short stories are in some sense political.

The point is that whatever we write from the personal perspective will reflect how we feel about matters moral, spiritual, ethical, social, and/or political. For the same reason that we try daily to be good people, true to ourselves and honest and generous with one another, we write truly, honestly, and generously: to make this planet a better home for ourselves and our fellow species.

I don't encourage, in fact I discourage, you from writing didactic, preachy fiction. But if you write truly about things you care about—and that I do encourage—then you will find yourself writing politics in some sense of the word. No matter how personal and small the moment of your story may be, be sure that it's significant; and to do that, first be a good person, and then be sure to write about what you care about.

What position should you take? Yours, of course. Beyond that there's not much one person can tell another, except to note that the best and most important political writing has always been critical of the establishment. There's virtually no point in writing to endorse the status quo, unless you're simply writing for the buck (television sitcoms, for example). We writers (and other artists) are the canaries in the mine shaft, and our songs are about the poisons we must breathe. Among the poisons are the censors (governmental or personal, yea, even ourselves) who would silence us. When we stop singing, the poisons will have won.

Finally let me say that if you decide to write "important" fiction, whether your stories be overtly political or personal with social overtones, whether you write about the garden of personal life or the jungle of society at large, remember that your first job is to write well. By writing about sociopolitical issues, you have decided to teach and even preach, but the way to do that in short fiction is to entertain. So select your scenes for the greatest story-telling force and write with style, have fun as you go forward, and give your reader a good time along with your important views of a better society.

STORIES ABOUT RELATIONSHIP

The word "relationship" can mean many things; in fact it's vague enough to mean just about anything where two or more anythings enjoy some sort of relativity. But for the purpose of this article, "relationship" refers to what goes on between two human beings. Specifically I'm referring to the dyad of love, the coupling that often (but not always) results in sex and/or marriage. The cast of characters is often (but not always) a woman and a man. Adam and Eve.

The relationship of Adam and Eve is perhaps the most common theme of short fiction. It also accounts for a good share of movies, plays, novels, and operas, and almost all popular songs. As for short fiction, I can think of no other theme or category more popular. Love, for short story writers and readers, and for almost everybody else, for that matter, makes the world go 'round.

(Love, as I've just illustrated, is also a minefield of clichés. I'll get to that later.)

It makes sense. We all come from coupling, and we all seek coupling or enjoy being coupled. We may enter this world alone, and we will departed it alone, but most of the time in between we're interested in, concerned with, often even obsessed by, the process of relationship. No wonder we need a break now and then—go to a movie, read a story. And no wonder so many movies and so many stories are about love.

The world "love," by the way, can name a wide range of emotions, including its own opposite, hate.

A relationship is made up of components physical, mental, and emotional. Body, mind and spirit, the triumvirate of elements that make us all human and define us individually as well.

I'll steer clear of defining the ideal relationship. Bookstore shelves are full of books that will tell you about successful relationship. If I knew how to make love work perfectly every time, I'd write one of those books and retire. But I don't know how to make love work right every time, or what makes a perfect, successful relationship. (I expect the authors of pop psychology don't either.) To tell you the truth, I don't think a perfectly happy relationship really exists, since any couple is made up of two less-than-perfect parts.

Furthermore, if a perfectly happy relationship did exist, it wouldn't make good fiction.

Plot requires conflict, and fiction about relationship focuses on the flaws in the relationship. Why is it we know nothing about the married life of Eve and Adam before they decided to break the rules? Because they were probably the one couple (unencumbered as they were by parents or former lovers) who had a perfect relationship, a relationship so happy it wasn't worth writing about. Perfectly dull. Their story only gets interesting with the introduction of relationship static: a tree of forbidden delights, a serpent seducer, a guilt-tripping God. At that point the story gets good—so good that we've been reenacting it ever since, in our fiction and in our lives.

Conflict in relationship fiction, as in real-life relationships, can come in an inexhaustible variety of forms.

All of us have had relationships, or at least have dreamed of having relationships. Furthermore, we've all read countless stories about relationship; our culture is soaking with relationship plots. So there's no excuse for not being inspired to write about relationship. We all have plenty of experience and ideas to work with.

The challenge is to do something original. And

being original is especially important in this arena.

Avoid clichés. Love is such a common experience, and fiction about love is so omnipresent in our culture, that we're tempted to rely on stereotypes and plot formulae. The lazy writer will use stale language ("heaving bosom," "pulsing manhood") or hackneyed situations ("My wife doesn't understand me." "You mean you're... *married?*") or stock characters (boy next door, whore with a heart of gold), and count on the reader to fill in the blanks. If ever there were a place to remember to show rather than tell, it's in the well-explored realm of relationship fiction, where the challenge is to find something original to say or an original way to say it.

Here's an essential rule for being original: Respect your characters as individuals. They're not just symbols or stereotypes or caricatures; they're people. Your reader must meet and spend time with them, so make your characters different and memorable, so that your reader will always remember them. This goes for the good guys and bad guys as well. If the woman is mean, make her mean in her own unique way; if she's kind, make it a special kindness we haven't seen before. And the more original they are, the realer they will be.

The same rule goes for your secondary characters: respect them as individuals. They're not just filling pages, they're real people too.

Having said that relationship fiction must focus on the problem areas in the relationship, let me now say that to make the story truly satisfying it should have some other elements as well. There should be more to the relationship than just the conflict, and there should be more to the story than just the relationship. These other elements, which may show up in the setting or the plot or the character development, will help make your story original.

Among the ingredients of any good short story are the elements of choice and change. These requirements are especially important in the area of relationship fiction. The characters, Adam and Eve, must make important choices, together and separately—to eat or not to eat, that is the question—and as a consequence of those choices, they will change as individuals and the relationship will change as well.

Since good fiction about relationship focuses on the problems in the relationship, the burning question (flaming brightly or smoldering quietly) is: can this marriage be saved? Will this couple make it? Will they fall apart and go separate ways? Will they be better off or worse off as a couple at the end of the story?

So the conflict in relationship fiction is not just between two lovers as adversaries, but between the couple and the circumstances.

ATMOSPHERIC STORIES

The environment of a story starts with physical description. It's called setting, or scene, or a sense of place. It's also called landscape, or stage. The writer must describe a piece of the universe. It's only a small piece of the real universe, of course, but while we're in the story (as writer or reader) that's all the universe we get, and so it represents the entire three-dimensional universe. It doesn't take much. To describe the force of a typhoon, you don't have to give a full weather report; a few details will suffice, if they're the right details.

The writer of the story is charged with the role of God: creator of the universe. Because stories are brief, and you the creator are an artist, you select carefully only a few parts of the universe to show in the story, parts that will make the scene seem complete to the reader. If you're successful, your reader will encounter in your story a place he or she may never have been before, and will recognize it immediately because of the details you select.

The physical setting of a story is created by what the characters perceive through the five senses: sight, hearing, smell, taste, and touch. Sight is the one we rely on most, but skillful writing demands that we use the others as well.

The physical details of the universe are only half of the story. Equally important, if not more important, is the mood of the place. Clearly the physical nature of the setting you describe will affect the mood of the characters in the story and influence what they do. In other words, the place will help propel the plot.

Less obviously, the mood of the characters helps to create the atmosphere of the story. This is a literary device called the pathetic fallacy. When King Lear gets lost in a tempest, that tempest is the outward manifestation of his dementia; it would not exist if the king hadn't lost it upstairs. You don't want to overplay the magic of the pathetic fallacy, but it is a handy trick, especially in fiction that stresses atmosphere.

Earlier I spoke of the universe as three-dimensional. That's only the beginning, for the universe has an important fourth dimension, that of time.

Short stories by their nature take us through a period of time, during which (by definition) something happens to someone. Something often also happens to the setting in which people change. In a story in which atmosphere is paramount, the environment is also likely to change.

The environment, or setting, or landscape, or atmosphere, or stage, or scene, or place, can change in either of two ways. The story can move from one location to another, beginning in Atlanta, for example, and ending in Brazil. But more often, in short fiction, the story stays in one setting and the setting itself changes, so that by the end of the story, it's not the same place it was when the story began.

Furthermore, the changes that happen to the environment are important. They affect the characters and they propel the plot, and sometimes they happen as a result of the characters and the plot. The changes nearly always reflect what the story is all about.

Dawn will break. The tempest will subside. Snow will fall.

In the meantime, things will have happened to people, from which they will never recover. Reacting to the changing physical and psychological atmosphere so dense around them, they will have made choices they can't take back.

HUMOROUS STORIES

Lighten up, I hear you cry. *Enough with all these sad stories already! Give us something to laugh at.*

Okay. Lessee. Okay. A guy slips on a banana peel and falls on his butt. No, wait. The guy's all dressed up, on his way to the career interview of a lifetime, and he slips on a banana peel and falls in a steaming pile of dog feces. Make that cat feces.

Did you hear the one about the man who was so poor he was reduced to eating his own shoes?

How about the woman who reads someone else's mail by accident, misunderstands, and thinks the man she loves is two-timing her. It breaks her heart.

This working-class married couple lives in an apartment in New York. They yell at each other constantly. Their best friends are neighbors, a couple that also yells at each other. Sometimes the two couples get together and they yell at each other. By the way, one of the men is obese, and both of the men frequently threaten their wives with violence.

So this salesman runs out of gas on a country road. A farmer takes him in for the night, but the salesman abuses the farmer's hospitality by seducing the farmer's teen-aged daughter, making her pregnant and ruining her life. The farmer forces the two strangers to get married at gunpoint, thereby ruining both of their lives.

There's this starving coyote, see. His prey eludes him and he accidentally runs off a cliff and falls thousands of feet to the rocks below.

A nice Italian or maybe Jewish or maybe both fruit vender is minding his own business when a gangster, a yuppie, and a cop all bash their cars into his pushcart, destroying his inventory and scattering all the money he's earned that week.

A homeless drunk needs to urinate so bad that he....

STOP!

What?

That stuff isn't funny.

Maybe I'm not telling it right. People have been laughing at this material forever.

It's not funny. It's sad.

I didn't say it wasn't sad. What do you think humor is, anyway?

Humor comes from sorrow, suffering, pain, cruelty, loneliness, and anger. Why is it all the Warner Brothers cartoon characters have speech impediments? What's funny about speech impediments? I don't know either, but those voices make us laugh. And speaking of cartoons, check out the topics covered by the comics in today's paper. An average day might serve up unruly children, meddlesome parents, nagging wives, boring husbands, divorce, overeating, poverty, taxes, crime, political corruption, sexual harassment, job stress, school stress, traffic accidents, sports accidents, phobias of all kinds, greed, jealousy, illnesses ranging from the common cold to Alzheimer's disease, and many different kinds of death, from shipwrecks to the electric chair. For starters. Real thigh-slappers.

There are two reasons not to be surprised that funny short stories originate in pain. First, good short stories must have conflict. Second, good short stories are about life, and life is full of pain. The Buddhists are right: the human condition is full of suffering.

So that's the bad news. The good news is that we have humor to help us carry the load. In fact, the humor can carry the load for us. Got a problem? Turn it into a joke. Why do so many overweight people, of all ages, laugh so much?

If suffering is essential to humor, so is surprise. Another word for surprise, when we're talking about skillful writing, is irony. Irony is a one-two punch. A good cop/bad cop routine. You set your reader up gently to expect one thing, and then *pow*. This device can work wonders at the sentence level, with twists of phrase that leave the reader reeling and rolling. Irony is even more important at the plot level, with events seeming to lead in one direction and ending up in another. Irony in a plot often involves the concept of karma or so-called poetic justice.

Another essential quality of good short fiction is originality: the humor has to be fresh. It's true that there are only a certain number of jokes in the world, and they've all been told before, but there is an endless source of fresh humor in our imaginations. Even when we deal with familiar ideas, we can be original.

Another essential ingredient of successful humorous short stories is intelligence. That should go without saying, but there's so much dumb humor in our culture, even dumb humor that's funny, that I make a special point of requiring intelligence before I'll call a short story good. It can't trade on its humor alone; it has to engage the brain, not just the funny bone. The story must be, on some level, about something that matters. Obviously a story is first and foremost a story, and its first job is to entertain. This is especially true of humorous stories. But if you don't give the reader something to think about, your story won't last in the memory any longer than a comic strip or a sitcom.

Finally, of course, a good humorous story requires style in spades. Why is it that all the jokes I told at the beginning of this discussion fell flat? No style. Zippo. Dullsville. Uma-Oprah time.

Everyone knows that the joke itself is only half the reason we laugh at a good comedian—if that. At least as important is the delivery. To tell a good joke you have to love language and practice daily all the many magic tricks you can do with it.

Become a magician and make your readers laugh so hard they hardly notice that they're crying as well.

EXPERIMENTAL STORIES

As I said at the end of the second chapter of this book, you may break the rules. In fact, you should break the rules. And when you break the rules, do so on purpose and out loud, because breaking the rules is part of what your story is about.

Does a plot sequence have to be made of consequential steps? Why can't it be just a series of seemingly unrelated events? Isn't that the charm of *Alice in Wonderland*? Does a plot have to be chronological? How about *The Alexandria Quartet,* which also experiments intriguingly with point of view? (I realize that these examples aren't drawn from the world of short fiction. I can break rules too.) Speaking of point of view, Ellen Gilchrist, one of the best short story writers at work today, head-hops constantly. In "Drunk With Love," the point of view shifts at the end of the story to a pair of unborn twins!

You don't have to write about significant matters. Many stories are about the sounds of words. Give yourself a treat and read Thomas Meehan's "Yma Dream."

As for language, you may forget everything you learned about being lean and strong; write as fancy as Nabokov or as dense as Faulkner if you think you can get away with it. Invent your own language, as Russell Hoban did for *Ridley Walker.* As I mentioned earlier, I once published an anthology of stories, each of which was only fifty-five words long. In one of the stories, each sentence was only one word long. In another of the stories, each word began with W.

Does a story have to hit the ground running? How about *Tristram Shandy,* which is almost half over before the main character is born? Does the climax have to come near the end? How about Kafka's *The Metamorphosis,* where the most important event in the book takes place just before the book begins?

Contrary to everything you've heard, an author may intrude and tell a reader what to think, may tell instead of show. That's what Updike does at the end of "Pigeon Feathers," and it works.

Yes, break rules, and remember the rule that every experiment is a success. That doesn't mean every experimental story you write will be publishable or even readable, but it does mean you will learn from having put the words on paper. In the meantime, you will have enjoyed the process.

Another rule is that you may return to the traditional whenever you want to. And you probably should, from time to time, if only for practice. Especially if you want to.

¶ Finding Your Audience

I believe there are three reasons a person might want to write short stories. They are (1) for the fun of it, (2) to communicate, and (3) to make money. I would like to discuss these three reasons in reverse order.

WRITING FOR MONEY

I've been a professional writer for thirty-five years now, off and on. In all that time I've earned less than twenty thousand dollars from my writing. Most of that was for ghostwriting; under my own name it's been more like five thousand dollars. Of that, $3500.00 was a grant I earned in 1967 (enough to support me for a year in those days). That leaves around $1500.00 earned from actually selling my words. I've had four books published by small presses and about seventy-five stories and articles published in magazines ranging from tiny to smallish, and have contributed chapters to two textbooks. I've also written a lot more that has never been published but took me just as much time to write. Obviously I don't write full time, but I've put enough time into all this product to bring my hourly rate to only a fraction of minimum wage. I've found that writing is no way for me to make a living.

Mine is not an unusually dismal experience. Most of the good writers that I know do not make a living solely from their writing, and none of them earn a living by writing short stories.

They do write, though, and so do you and so do I. Because we couldn't not write. It's the way we organize our thoughts and emotions, the way we process life and the universe. It's satisfying, if not lucrative.

WRITING TO COMMUNICATE

But lonely. Writing is the loneliest of art forms. An actor knows right away whether he or she has done a good job. A painter can watch the expressions on the faces of the people who look at his or her work. Musicians get energy back from each other and from the applause of their audience. But a writer works in a vacuum and then waits for a long time, sometimes forever, before finding out if the thing worked, made contact.

You can go crazy this way, and the harder you work the crazier you'll get.

That's why it's important for a writer to find an audience. It's not for the money (short story writers don't make money), it's not for the fame (ditto get famous), it's for the completion of the job. Contact. Communication.

Writing is an art, and art implies communication. Reason number two for being a writer.

So get yourself an audience. Join groups. Take classes. Attend and participate in open readings. Swap stories on the Internet. Read to one another in covens. Correspond with your cousin in Milwaukee who also writes. Find a mentor and be a mentor. Subscribe to literary magazines.

Send your work out. Publish!

A LOOK AT THE SHORT STORY MARKET

The news here is not all good. Once upon a time a short story writer could make a decent living churning out tales and sending them off to the pulps because there were hundreds of magazines publishing thousands of short stories for millions of readers, and those magazines paid their writers! Then came television. Don't get me started.

Now there are only a handful of mass-distribution magazines in the United States that pay their writers more than a hundred bucks for a story, and they publish only a handful of stories by a handful writers, most of whom already have earned literary reputations as successful novelists.

Your chances of getting rich or famous by selling

short stories are not as good as your chances of winning a lottery.

But wait. There is good news. Every year, judging from the steady weight-gain of the *Novel and Short Story Writers' Market,* there are more and more magazines that do publish short fiction. They may not pay big bucks, and they may have small circulations, but they're there, and they do print stories, and they will read your work, and if your work is right for them it will have a home. Someone out there will read and enjoy what you have enjoyed writing.

So get yourself a copy of *Novel and Short Story Writers' Market,* keep it in the bathroom with a yellow highlighter, and read it for pleasure. You will certainly find there many intriguing markets, and those are the markets most likely to be intrigued by your work.

HOW TO GET PUBLISHED

You need three ingredients to get published. (And by "published," I do not mean in *Playboy* or *The New Yorker*; I mean in the hundreds of small literary magazines who will actually read what you submit.) Those three ingredients are talent, hard work, and luck.

Let us assume that you have talent. Have faith in that. It's like having faith in the hereafter or in the goodness of our friends. We have to have faith, whether it's justified or not. And we have to work to justify that faith. Assuming that we have talent, we must practice it to keep it in shape. That leads us to hard work.

Hard work is hardly work, because we're doing it for the fun of it, but nonetheless we must work honestly and diligently to come up with a product that's worth publishing. I know one writer and teacher who insists we should all write one thousand words a day. Works for her. Not all of those words will find their way into print, but it keeps a writer practicing the craft, and some of the words will be the ones that land in place.

As for luck, you can influence the odds simply by playing the game with all your chips as often as you can. Having worked hard and produced at least a dozen good stories, stories that you'd be proud to see in print, get those stories out in the mail. And for each of them, be ready with another addressed envelope and cover letter, so that when it comes back (it usually will), it won't sit around going sour. It will go out again, to another fortunate editor. With twelve stories out in the mail all year long, you're going to get read by as many as a hundred different editors, and one of them, sometime, somewhere, will like something you've written. Bingo.

Keep a ledger of where your stories have been.

Do your homework about where to send your stories. Find out what magazines are interested in, either by reading their entries in *Novel and Short Story Writers' Market* or by browsing libraries and bookstores and even buying and reading an issue or two. Who knows? Maybe you have a story set in a laundromat, and maybe there's a magazine dedicated to laundromat fiction? That's far-fetched, but there are magazines about juggling, UFOs, Kansas, jazz, lesbians, just about all religious sects, and a host of other special interests that might be part of your stories.

In any case, don't waste time and postage by sending stories to magazines for whom they're clearly inappropriate. Obey the instructions in the guidelines concerning format and length.

Neatness counts.

Always enclose a self-addressed, stamped envelope (SASE) if you want to hear back. Magazines are poor, and editors are justifiably stingy with their time and money. Besides, you should be professional and polite, and that means enclose a SASE.

Write back to editors when they reject you, especially if they invite you to send something else. But don't ever argue with them or ask them to read the same story again. It will do you no good, and it will probably do you harm. Don't bug magazine editors over the phone.

Write lots of letters to people you've never met. Letters to authors you admire. Write to agents, to publishers, to book reviewers, to magazine editors, just to let the world know that you're a writer too. Without being an apple-polisher, let the world of short story writers know who you are, so that they'll want to read what you write. Believe me, this will pay off eventually, and in the meantime you may make some new friends.

Finally, reason number one for wanting to write short stories: to have fun doing it. The very act of writing short stories should give you the most pleasure you can imagine getting from that moment. Do not write short stories for money; you'll be disappointed. Do not write them for fame or praise. Write to give yourself a good time. Given the difficulty of making money or even communicating, you have to really love the process of writing to be happy doing it.

If writing short fiction isn't a great pleasure for you, then my advice to you is to do that other thing that is your favorite pleasure: macramé, tinker with your car, whatever. This will be a wonderful world when we all get to do what we love doing most. Until then we're satisfying someone else at best, and at worst, wasting our time.

But if you've read this far, chances are you are a real writer, and you love short stories. So you will write on, and it will make you happy, even if it drives you nuts in the process.

The short story writer is someone who must write short stories, just as painters must paint and actors must act. We are addicted to the joy of making up people and plots, choosing the right words and placing them in the right order, so that something will happen to somebody.

To borrow Rust Hills's words once more, that is the joy of fiction in general and the short story in particular.